Sara's Secret

by Suzanne Wanous
illustrated by Shelly O. Haas

Carolrhoda Books, Inc./Minneapolis

Special thanks to Bobbi Hoppman, Project Coordinator for Nekton, Inc., which provides support services to children and adults with developmental disabilities.

Text copyright © 1995 by Suzanne Wanous
Illustrations copyright © 1995 by Shelly O. Haas

Carolrhoda Books, Inc. c/o The Lerner Group
241 First Avenue North, Minneapolis, MN 55401

LIBRARY OF CONGRESS CATALOGING-IN-PUBLICATION DATA

Wanous, Suzanne
   Sara's secret / by Suzanne Wanous ; illustrated by Shelly O. Haas
    p. cm.
   Summary: At first Sara doesn't want anyone at her new school to know about her younger brother Justin who has cerebral palsy.
   ISBN: 0-87614-856-9
   [1. Cerebral palsy—Fiction. 2. Mentally handicapped—Fiction.
3. Physically handicapped—Fiction. 4. Brothers and sisters—
Fiction. 5. Moving, Household—Fiction. 6. Schools—Fiction.]
I. Haas, Shelly O., ill. II. Title.
PZ7.W1817Sar 1995
[Fic]—dc20

                    94-32234
                       CIP
                       AC

Manufactured in the United States of America
1 2 3 4 5 6 - I/JR - 00 99 98 97 96 95

To my beloved family,
who read, listened, and believed.

To Christopher,
your parents' love and your own special way of giving
have changed my life forever.

To all my students,
I believe you taught me as much as I taught you.
—S.W.

To charity out of love with gestures
that multiply by expression.

With special thanks to
Peri, Rachel, Janet, and Randi,
for inspiration and reality.

And especially to Dillon,
who was there when no one else could be.
—S.O.H.

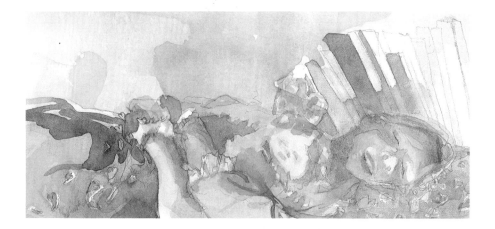

Mornings are hectic at our house. Mom hurries off to work before I'm even awake, and Dad's always busy getting Justin ready for school. Sometimes Dad forgets to wake me up on time, so I barely have a chance to gulp down my cereal before running to catch the bus. In the afternoons, Mom takes care of Justin while Dad works late. You see, Justin isn't like other five-year-olds. His mind and his body are handicapped. He needs help doing everything.

Justin's special education bus comes right to our house at 8:25. Every morning Dad says, "Sara, why don't you ride with Justin?" He thinks I would be a big help by taking Justin to his classroom on the way to mine. But I always leave early and run up the long, empty lane to catch the regular bus at 8:15. When I get to school, I usually see Justin's bus driver putting him on the lift to get his wheelchair off the bus. She waves whenever she sees me. I never used to wave back. She knows Justin's my brother, but for a while last fall, no one else did. I wanted it that way.

I'd only been at this school for a few weeks. My family had just moved here. I didn't want the new kids to tease Justin and me like they did at our old school. They called Justin a retard and said I might be one too. Nobody understood that even though my brother can't walk or talk or feed himself, or even sit up, he can still make me happy. He likes it when I rub my cheek against his or when I play a game with him. Sometimes he stops what he's doing and looks around to find me. He smiles when he sees my face. Mom says he sure knows I'm his special sister.

The new school seemed okay until Mr.
Hernandez, my teacher, announced that
we'd be talking about disabilities. He
started by asking what we could tell him.
"A disability is when you can't walk," Tina
said.

"It's something you can't do very well,
like talking," said Steven. I started to feel
better. I thought maybe these kids would
understand about Justin after all.

But then Billy said, "A lot of the kids in

the special ed class are slobbery. I hate that." Then other kids started saying bad things, too. Joshua said he was afraid of them, and Gwen said she didn't like to look at them in the hallway.

The worst part was that Mr. Hernandez didn't even say they were wrong. He just gave us an assignment to think of one thing that would help a person with disabilities. If we could bring something to class, that was even better.

My friends Tina and Kimberly talked about the assignment on the way to the bus after school. "I'd like to bring my grandmother's hearing aid," Tina said, "but I don't think she'd let me. She can barely hear me talking right into her ear without it."

Kimberly asked me what I was going to do. I shook my head, "I can't think of anything." As we headed toward the bus, I saw Justin in his wheelchair waiting to be lifted onto his bus. I looked away.

But the driver saw me and called, "Come on! I'll take you home. It's starting to rain." I pretended I didn't hear her and got on the regular bus so fast I knocked Mary over on the steps. She yelled that I should wait my turn, but I didn't care. I sat in the back and watched the rain pour down the windows all the way to my stop.

When I got home, Mom frowned as I took off my soaked shoes. I grabbed a couple of warm ginger cookies from the counter and said hello to Justin. "I don't understand why you won't ride Justin's bus at least on days like this," Mom said.

I shrugged and took a bite of cookie.

"Mmmm. Good!" I told Justin, holding it close to his face so he could smell the warm, spicy scent. Mom had put a cookie in a special grinder to make it soft enough for him to swallow. She fed him tiny bites. The brown mush ran out of his mouth with each bite, and Mom wiped it up before it dribbled onto his shirt. Mom asked about my day, so I told her about the puppets we made in art class. I knew she'd want to hear about my assignment, but I wasn't sure I wanted to tell her. She didn't know I was keeping Justin a secret.

When Justin had finished his cookie,
Mom started reading the note from Justin's
teacher. His teacher writes every day to tell
us what he did in class. Today, he must
have finger painted, because a sticky, purple
and yellow paper was attached to the note.

"We're kind of doing a lesson on
disabilities," I blurted out. I hadn't even
decided if I wanted to tell her, and right
away I was sorry I had.

Mom stopped reading and looked up.

"You should have a lot to say, Sara. You could almost teach the class!"

"I guess I just have to bring something that helps Justin," I said quickly. "It's about all different kinds of handicaps."

"Maybe you could bring his food grinder, or you could go to his class and get his wheelchair. Say, I'll bet Justin's teacher would let you bring *him* to your class if I wrote her a note. . . ." I pretended I couldn't hear the rest and went to get another cookie.

After dinner, Mom put Justin in his sidelyer, which helps him lie on his side to play with his toys. Without it he falls onto his back with his arms at his sides. It also stretches his back muscles. It's supposed to be comfortable, but Justin doesn't like it. He was making a quiet whimpering noise. When Mom left the room, I put my face by Justin's warm cheek. "You don't mind that I keep you a secret, do you?" I whispered. Justin stopped fussing and smiled. That

made me feel even worse. I stayed and played with him until Mom got him out of the sidelyer.

When Mom tucked me in that night, she sat on the edge of my bed and asked me if I'd thought about what to bring to school.

"I'm not sure," I said, pretending to be really tired. Mom looked sad as she kissed me and turned out the light. When Dad came home, he came in to say good night. I pretended I was asleep, but I wasn't.

"Good morning, sweetheart," Dad said cheerfully the next morning. He woke me up right on time, but this time I wished I could stay in bed. "Mom told me about your assignment," Dad said at breakfast. "She didn't know if you wanted to bring Justin to your class, but I can write a note for his teacher if you want me to."

I didn't want him to, but I didn't want him to feel bad, either. "Sure, I guess so," I said. I watched drool run down Justin's chin onto his clean shirt as Dad fed him some cereal. "There's no way I would bring you to my class, Justin," I said very, very quietly.

Justin looked up. He must have heard his name. Dad handed me the note, and I shoved it into my pocket as I walked out the door.

The kids brought a lot of different things to class. Jill borrowed a white cane from a friend who was blind. Kimberly brought a library book on sign language. And Tina's grandmother let her bring her hearing aid. Tina carefully guarded its tiny box.

I had trouble concentrating all morning. Finally after lunch, I heard what I'd been dreading. Mr. Hernandez said it was time to talk more about disabilities. They all were excited to show what they'd brought, but my stomach felt sick. I jumped up and whispered in the teacher's ear that I had to leave the room.

I stood trembling in the hall between my room and Justin's. I felt Dad's note in my pocket. I thought about how bad I felt when the kids teased me at the other school. If I didn't tell the class about Justin, it would mean I was ashamed of him. If I did, they might tease me for the rest of the year. I crumpled the note between my fingers. I thought about Justin's smile and how he loved me just for being near him. He was my brother, not a secret.

Meghan was telling the class about the brace on her cousin's knee when I walked back into my classroom. Some kids turned and stared. Justin was with me in his wheelchair. I wanted to hide. I wanted to turn around and take him back. But when Meghan sat down, I wheeled Justin to the front of the room. I turned my brother's wheelchair so he could see all the kids and they could see him.

"Sometimes," I began, looking at the floor, my voice shaking, "having a disability means you can't walk or talk or even feed yourself. This is Justin." I nuzzled my cheek against his, and he smiled a great big smile. I felt a little better. I dared to look at the class. "Justin is my brother." No one looked disgusted, though some, especially Tina and Kimberly, looked surprised.

Some of the kids started asking questions. "Why are his arms and legs so stiff?" "How does he eat?" "Do you play together?"

I tried to answer them all. "Justin didn't get enough oxygen when he was born, so he has cerebral palsy and is mentally retarded. Cerebral palsy means he can't control his muscles very well, and it's hard for him to move them. His teachers and therapist work with him every day to help make him stronger. Justin eats most of the same foods I eat, but mushed up." I told them how I make up games to play with him, and if he likes them, he smiles, or relaxes and leans on me. And if he doesn't like them, he cries and his body tightens up.

"He has a lot of problems learning," I said, "but we teach him and he teaches us how to understand each other better. But even though he's learning a lot, Justin won't be able to read or write . . . ever."

There was an uncomfortable silence, and I wasn't sure what to say next. Mr. Hernandez took over. "When Justin was born and didn't have enough oxygen, part of his brain was hurt. This part of his brain doesn't work now." He told the class how sometimes just a little of the brain is hurt, and a child will be mildly retarded. When a lot of the brain is injured, a child will be profoundly retarded, like Justin. "Kids often use the term 'retard' or 'mentally retarded' to insult each other," he said. Some of the kids laughed at that. Mr. H. wrote "mentally retarded" on the board.

He turned back to the class. "These words may make you laugh or feel uncomfortable. But try to get comfortable with them. They really tell you only a little bit about a person. You have to get to know them to find out what they're really like."

I glanced at Justin to make sure he wasn't drooling. He wasn't. I wondered how he liked being in front of the class. He was looking at me as if he were trying to see how I felt. I smiled, and he smiled right back. I could tell he was interested in the faces around him. He looked at them carefully while struggling to keep his head up straight. I put my hand on his head to keep it steady, and he relaxed and looked from face to face.

Then Joel asked the question I was most afraid of. "Isn't he one of the kids who slobbers?" I looked at Mr. Hernandez for help. He was waiting for my answer, too.

"Yes, he slobbers," I began slowly. "I know it looks yucky, but my mom says his mouth muscles can't swallow and keep his lips closed at the same time." Joel giggled. Joshua said he'd better be careful or else he'd catch cerebral palsy.

Mr. H. spoke up quickly. He explained that there's a difference between an illness we can catch and a disability. He told us that a disability can be caused by many things, such as an injury or a disease. But an illness is caused by germs. "We all know that we can catch germs from each other," he said, "but we can't catch a disability. We can't catch cerebral palsy."

When class was over, I was actually kind of disappointed to take Justin back to his room. In the hall between our classrooms, I stopped and looked at Justin. "Well, buddy," I said, "that wasn't so bad, huh? Now everyone knows you're my brother." I thought of how Joel and Joshua had giggled. I wondered what Kimberly and Tina thought.

"How did it go?" Justin's teacher asked me.
"It was okay," I said. I held Justin's face
so he'd look right at me. "It went okay,
didn't it?" I nuzzled his cheek, and he gave
me a big smile.

At the end of the day, Kimberly looked through her sign language book while we waited for the bus. "I never knew you had a brother," Tina said.

"Yeah, why didn't you tell us?" Kimberly echoed, looking up from her book.

I shrugged my shoulders. How could I tell them I didn't think they would still be my friends? "Hey," I said, changing the subject. "Do you want to come over after school tomorrow?" Tina said yes right away.

Kimberly didn't answer. She paged through her book while I held my breath. When she found what she was looking for, she made a fist and shook it up and down. "Yes," she said. We laughed, but I was relieved. I turned and watched as Justin's wheelchair was lifted onto the special education bus. "See you at home, Justin!" I called to him.

Author's Note

As Sara explained to her class, cerebral palsy, or CP, is caused by damage to the part of the brain that controls the muscles of the body. This brain damage can happen in different ways, although in many cases, doctors do not know why a child's brain did not develop normally. CP sometimes results when a mother has a serious illness during her pregnancy, when a baby doesn't get enough air before or during birth, or when a very young child has an illness or injury. Justin has a severe form of CP. People with milder forms of CP can often learn to walk and run and do many things others can do.

Justin is also mentally retarded. Not everyone with cerebral palsy is mentally retarded. Mental retardation has a number of causes. Like CP, it can happen before birth, when part of the brain does not grow completely or when a pregnant mother is very ill. Drugs or alcohol that a mother takes during pregnancy can also hurt her baby. Mental retardation can be passed from parents to children, just like brown eyes or curly hair. Mental retardation can also be caused by an injury or illness anytime after a child is born. As with CP, the effects of mental retardation can be mild to severe.

Even though Justin is severely mentally retarded and can't communicate by talking, his family and teachers use other ways to communicate with him. Learning about cerebral palsy and mental retardation can help us to understand these disabilities and then, most importantly, get to know people like Justin and Sara who live with them.